WARNING

This book contains sexually explicit scenes and adult language. It may be considered offensive to some readers. This book is for sale to adults ONLY.

* * * * * * * * * * * * * * * * *

Please store your files wisely where they cannot be accessed by underage readers.

ISBN-13: 978-1987863994
ISBN-10: 1987863992

Other Books by Darla Dunbar:

<u>The Romeo Alpha BBW Paranormal Shifter</u>
<u>Romance Series</u>

Amanda Walker thinks that she has a normal and boring life. That is until after her 24th birthday. Everything changes when she meets the man who says he was supposed to be her husband. Denying everything the man says, she fights him every step of the way. But after he kidnaps her, Amanda discovers that there are some things about her family that her parents kept a secret all these years. Among the history of the family she learns secrets she thought only happened in story books. Can Amanda tell the difference between truth and lies or is she this mysterious woman that holds the key to a legacy?

<u>Romeo Alpha Blood Lines Romance Series</u>

Twenty-four years have passed in relative peace for Amanda and Romeo. They've raised five children into adulthood and are thoroughly enjoying their lives as the Alpha King and Queen of the werewolves. At twenty-four, Sarina is just stepping into her powers and will be ripe for mating when her birthday comes in two weeks. What no one knows is the danger that lurks just outside their tight knit community. Romeo has made peace with the other clans and has enjoyed that peace, but it will all come crashing down around him when his oldest daughter comes of age to take a mate.

The Alpha Feud BBW Paranormal Shifter Romance Series

Eliza's life consisted of reporting on boring, crowd-pleasing events, like their country livestock fair. With the arrival of two handsome brothers, the lives of Eliza and her best friend, Melissa, are shaken to the core. For Eliza, the arrival of this new man becomes a test of her relationship with her current boyfriend, who she's been happily living with for over six years. Does Hayden, a complete stranger, really wield the power to make Eliza reconsider her relationship with Andrew?

The Alpha Packed BBW Paranormal Shifter Romance Series

Darlene has led a quiet life since suffering through a terrible break-up. She wants nothing more than to spend her time in front of the TV, away from any sort of trouble. But all that goes down the drain when handsome, rugged and rough Idris comes into her life. He is a werewolf on the lookout for his missing pack leader. Darlene quickly finds herself pulled towards this mysterious man and at the same time finds herself falling deeper and deeper into the world of the supernatural.

The Daemon Paranormal Romance Chronicles

The daemon infighting can only be stopped when a strong leader emerges to calm the different factions. Juno appears to be at the heart of the conflict. Things become complicated when Phoebe and Supay try to negotiate with the siren, Juno. The love triangle among Phoebe, Supay and Apollo become tense when Juno's meddling threatens to destroy any romance that develops.

<u>The Leather Satchel Paranormal Romance Series</u>

Valtina is stuck in Middle World, unable to pass on to The Afterlife. In order to redeem herself from past deeds done, she must help bring romance back into the world and stop The Dark Side from destroying love in its entirety. Following orders issued by Ladaya and armed with a leather satchel filled with the appropriate tools and weapons, Valtina embraces each mission with enthusiasm.

Get the latest update on new releases from the author at:

https://darladunbar.com/newsletter/

This book is Part Four of the "The Mind Talker Paranormal Romance Series"

Book 1 - Awareness

Ananda discovered that she can read other people's mind when she was 11. It is supposed to be a gift but it's driving her crazy. Lonely and disoriented, Ananda runs off to New York. She thinks that in a city as big as that, there must be someone like her walking around. One day, man's voice calls out to her. The strange thing is that she heard the voice in her mind.

Book 2 - Hunted

Jared's past haunted him and served as a reminder that he can't escape his fate. If he had stopped the boy back then, would his sister still be alive? Jenny was the love of Jared's life until he discovered she was living a double life. Jenny was part of a secret organization that was bent on hunting him.

Book 3 - Heat

Ananda couldn't help herself. Jared's scent just sends her over the edge. No one else understood Ananda's gift... not even her parents. When Jared found Ananda, he explained what her special powers meant. Only certain people acquired the gift of reading minds. Along with that, Ananda was undergoing a maturation process. Every one of her kind will experience it in their 21st year.

Book 4 - Revealed

Jared learns the truth about his dead sister. Ananda had the power to see into his past. She saw what he saw during that fateful day when Jared's sister died. Meanwhile, the truth about Kerri's family is revealed. They are the sole reason why Ananda and her kind are on the endangered list.

Book 5 - Evasion

Ryan is the mystery man who is helping Jared and Ananda to escape to Canada in hopes of evading the organization that is hunting all those with special mind reading powers. Kerri's family is behind the secret organization. Her love for Ryan has forced her to choose between loyalty to family and loyalty to Ryan. Can she be trusted?

The Mind Talker Paranormal Romance Series

Revealed

Book Four

By Darla Dunbar

Copyright Revelry Publishing 2015

Table of Contents

Chapter One

JARED WAS quiet for the next few hours as they continued their drive. He hadn't responded when Ananda explained that she had seen his sister and the message she had given her. The idea that not only had Sophie known about her brother's gift but somehow also had the gift herself was alarming and Ananda just knew that asking questions now would be a bad move. So rather than talk and risk upsetting the man further, Ananda decided to catch up on as much sleep as possible. She was still unsure of their destination and secretly she was terrified that the dark figure from her vision would find them before they reached whatever destination they were heading to.

"I'm sorry." The sound of Jared's voice was almost overly loud in the quiet of the car. Ananda opened her eyes but refused to turn around. Somehow she knew that whatever the man needed to say, it would be much easier for him to get it out if she weren't looking at him. "I'm not angry with you…it's just…" Jared paused, as if to gather courage. "The whole time we were growing up, Sophie never ever told me she had a gift. Not even when I started hearing voices and told her. I always thought that if I had done more, I could have saved her that day. If only I had told someone about Kevin instead of hiding away like a coward. Or if I had stayed in the cafeteria that day…"

"Then you would have died along with everyone else and you wouldn't have been here, now, alive and able to keep me from being caught or killed by whoever is after me!" Ananda couldn't help but turn to look at the man. The sound of his grief was almost more than she could bear. "I didn't know your sister, but I'm sure she would never have wanted you to be there that day. She was your big sister and for some reason… for some reason that I just can't explain, I know she knew what was going to happen."

If not for his iron grip on the steering wheel, Jared might have jerked out of his seat with shock. "What?" He couldn't wrap his head around the thought. Even if Sophie had had the gift, she wasn't old enough for extra abilities to have manifested. "She wasn't old enough to have that ability. Abilities like that don't manifest until after maturation."

"I know... I know you said that but… I don't know how to explain it Jared." She put her hand softly on Jared's shoulder, willing him to understand what she saw and felt. Suddenly a tingling sensation manifested almost like an itch behind her ear. The feeling traveled down her arm and into the tips of her fingers as they rested against Jared's warm skin until she was sure that the man had to be feeling something. It was odd how surely Ananda felt about Jared when they had only met one another seventy-two hours ago. She spared a thought for Kerri and wondered what her dearest friend was doing in her absence. "Do you think I could call

Kerri, or my parents? I mean, would it be safe to call them? They aren't in any danger, right?"

Jared thought carefully before he decided what to say. "Ananda, how much do you know about your roommate Kerri?" he questioned, glancing over at the girl before reaffixing his focus back to the desolate road in front of him. Thankfully they had made good time getting out of the city and were close enough to their first stop in Rochester that he felt he could relax just a little. Jared hadn't been looking forward to cluing Ananda in to who her friend really was, or the family that she left behind, but he knew that in order to keep the woman he had come to care for safe, he needed to be completely honest and if that meant divulging some uncomfortable truths then so be it.

On her end, Ananda was struck dumb by the question. "What do you mean? I know she comes from a big family and has, I think, two or three brothers and sisters. Her dad was a real piece of work though and he treated them all terribly." She couldn't figure out why Jared was so intent on information about Kerri.

"Did any of them ever visit you guys at school? Did you ever meet her family even once?" Jared glanced over quickly again noting the woman's perplexed expression. "Think carefully, Ananda. This is important. Did you ever meet any of Kerri's family?"

"No I…" Ananda tried to think back over the past three years of her and Kerri's friendship. She remembered meeting Kerri randomly at one of the freshman activities and being in awe at first of the other girl's exuberant personality and then later relieved at the quietness of her mind. Despite the fact that they had shared almost three full years together, first as friends and then as roommates, not once did she ever meet the other girl's family. In fact, regardless of all the times she brought Kerri back to meet her family, there was never a reciprocated offer. It was as if Kerri's family life was completely separate from her life at school with Ananda. The realization made something heavy settle into her gut and she wondered how she could've been so blind as to not be suspicious that in all the time she'd known Kerri, not once had she thought to question it. It made her heart beat faster at the thought of Kerri being somehow involved with the people chasing them. What if it had been Kerri who let the person into their apartment?

"She didn't."

Ananda was startled by Jared's voice breaking her inner dialogue of betrayal and confusion. Slowly she looked up until their eyes met, hers shining with the moisture of unshed tears in the face of her best friend's possible duplicity.

"She didn't betray you, Ananda. This I know for a fact," Jared could still feel the woman's simmering feelings of sadness and hurt.

"How do you know?" Ananda looked down as her hands tightened into fists. How could she have been so stupid? A large strong hand came over and settled on top of hers; a thumb rubbing the back of one hand until she forced them to relax. Taking a deep breath, Ananda tangled her fingers with Jared's, trying not to blush at her boldness but feeling the need to be close and seek comfort.

"Because she told me, or she thought it at me rather," Jared stumbled over his wording trying his best to comfort Ananda and yet make her see what they were up against. "In all the time you have known her, not once have you been able to get a read on her thoughts, just vague emotions right?"

"Yeah."

"And she never took you to meet her family or invited them over when you were around?"

"Yeah… no, never. She made it seem like there had been a falling out or something. Like maybe she was estranged from them I think, something about her not living up to her father's expectations. She was always really angry about it and yet totally vague. Though…honestly, I think it might have been because of a high school boyfriend… her dad didn't approve and kept them apart…" Ananda trailed off unsure as Jared nodded to himself. He'd always wondered how the organization that hunted people like them continued to operate, targeting younger and younger subjects.

"Look, remember the organization I talked about that is hunting people like us? Well, it's her family or rather they were her family if what you said is true about her being estranged. I was kind of surprised to see you two so close given who or what she is, but it definitely makes sense. Her father probably hunted that boyfriend of hers and that's what the catalyst of the estrangement was. Perhaps we can use your relationship…"

"No!" Ananda jerked her hands back away from Jared's and turned away. Everything in her life had been so perfect until this gift of hers fucked it all up.

"Ana, I'm not saying that we should take advantage of Kerri or anything, but it's clear that she loves you like a sister and I'm sure she doesn't want us getting caught or you getting hurt. She probably blames herself right now for not telling you who she really was."

"I don't," Ananda swallowed hard against the lump in her throat, desperately trying to hold back the tears that threatened to fall as she watched the trees go passing by. She could hear the sound of Jared shifting in his seat, but was still caught by surprise when his arm lay softly across her shoulder.

"Then we won't, okay?" Breathing deeply, Jared decided to just go with what he was feeling instead of trying to fight or hide it. "I want to protect you using any means possible and I know your friend Kerri wants to do the same. For now we'll just worry about getting as far away as possible before deciding our next move. I have a few contacts in Toronto who can help us set up new identities and new lives which should hopefully keep us off the radar for a good long while."

"But, what will I tell my parents? How will I finish school?" Ananda sat up, eyes red-rimmed from her tears as she thought about all the hard work she had done over the past three years. Truthfully, she had been undecided on her major and had only recently decided to stick with psychology, but the thought of abandoning her life… the life she had had for twenty-one years, was enough to send her into a panic. Ananda clenched her hands into fists. 'Fuck, I'm not going to cry again!' She had just stopped her tears and already they were threatening to overwhelm her again. Her heart started to once again beat unsteadily and what little food she had eaten at the last rest stop was threatening to make a reappearance in a hurry. She already lost her parents once when her gifts had manifested the first time. She didn't want to lose them again, or her brother Ryan. And then what about Kerri and the other friends she had made at the university? True, she hadn't really bothered to keep in touch with those friends as much, and it had been months since she had been in touch with Ryan or her parents. Oh God, what if everything had been going this way for a reason. Maybe her parents would be happier with her gone?

Suddenly, Ananda's chest went tight and she gasped, unable to slow her breathing. She ground her teeth together to brace herself for the panic attack she knew was bearing down on her with startling quickness. Distantly Ananda could hear Jared's voice calling out to her, his hand cupping her cheek. Her body began to shake uncontrollably and it felt like the world suddenly tilted on its axis as Jared roughly jerked the wheel, turning into a motel parking lot. Dimly Ananda was aware of the passenger side door being opened and her body being lifted out, Jared carrying her bridal-style into a dimly lit room and locking the latch behind him. She could only barely breathe as her body refused to cease its shaking. Her head was pounding as Ananda curled into a fetal position wishing that someone would just put her out of her misery.

Instead she got Jared's voice, gruff and yet soft, whispering sweet things into her ear that she had no hope of understanding while she was in her panicked state. She could feel a hand running gingerly through her hair, stopping to massage at her temples and sending calming feelings in their wake. The panic began to fade, leaving the hurt behind as Ananda became more aware of her surroundings. She could feel Jared curled up behind her, his warmth and scent doing wonders at calming her down.

"It's okay my love," Jared whispered, voice soft and soothing to Ananda's shot nerves. "We'll be okay. Just relax and sleep. I'll be here for you when you wake and we'll figure out together what to do. Just trust me and let go." For a moment Ananda considered fighting back and raging, but the warmth and concern in the man's voice lessened the terrible pressure in her aching chest and soon enough sleep claimed her for its own.

Jared watched over Ananda while she slept. Her panic attack brought on by realizing that everything she had ever known was gone had riled Jared more than he let on. Truthfully, she wasn't the only one who would have to let go of the life she had once known. He'd never be able to visit his parents and grieve together or visit Sofie's grave without worrying that someone might spot him. His parents would have to deal with the pain of essentially losing both of their children, which wasn't something he had ever let himself think about even after he'd become aware of the organization that was hunting him. Somewhere in the back of his mind he had hoped that it was all just a big misunderstanding, but now he realized that his desire to have life remain the same may be what was hindering him from moving on. Looking down at Ananda's sleep tossed hair and forlorn expression even in sleep made something powerful bloom in his chest. He would do anything for this woman, and if that meant abandoning the life he'd known then so be it. He knew that with Ananda by his side, he could build a better future and work towards one day not having to look over his shoulder or hide his abilities. He could learn to love himself and maybe even find a happiness greater than what he had ever known. Shifting, Jared extended his mind out to see if anyone had been tailing them. All he heard were some rather inappropriate conversations and prayers and so he allowed himself to relax slightly. He knew he wouldn't be able to fully let himself unwind until they were across the border and safely ensconced in his friend Bill's safe house. For now he would give himself a moment's reprieve to enjoy the closeness he shared with Ananda.

Chapter Two

The feeling of shifting and long heavy sighs woke Jared up a few hours later and he tightened the arm that was draped around Ananda's waist. "Again?" he intoned sleepily, nose buried behind Ananda's ear and taking in the honey sweetness that was starting to waft from her. Truly he didn't mind being woken up by her need for sex; if anything he hoped that it would become a regular sort of thing in their lives. Reaching up, Jared turned Ananda's head slightly, enough to where he could capture her already bite-reddened lips with his own. The kiss started out innocent enough until Ananda's groan sent over pleasant vibrations that turned the kiss into something deeper and more passionate. Soon enough, Jared found himself kneeling above Ananda, one arm propping him up while the other tried its damndest to rid them of their clothing. Ananda parted her lips in order to allow Jared's tongue to stroke over her own as her legs fell further apart. Her hands came up, one clasping Jared's upper arm in a tight grip while the other hand ran slight fingernails over the man's back.

Jared broke away gasping for breath and shuddering hard at the sensation of Ananda's nails against his skin. Leaning down, he shifted slightly in order to suck stinging kisses into the skin of Ananda's neck.

"Jared," Ananda moaned, hips shifting and raising. Upon contact with Jared's tightened body, she let out a louder groan grinding against him in tight circles. Jared answered with a bite to Ananda's collarbone as he fought to keep himself from thrusting back and ending things too prematurely.

Ananda tried again to draw his attention to the place she really needed it. "Jared, come on. Please touch me. God at least get my pants off and your pants off. I'd really like to be naked so I can come…and then make you come…repeatedly." Jared made a hungry noise in the back of his throat before rocking back to perch on his heels. He unbuttoned Ananda's jeans and moved slowly back, peeling them off as he went. Slowly Ananda's overheated skin was revealed to the cooler heat of the room. She shivered slightly as goose bumps rose on her sensitive skin. He trailed his lips down the woman's body, stopping occasionally to linger over a spot that made Ananda's back arch with pleasure. Soon his open-mouthed and wet kisses slid to the skin of her inner thigh and breathing deeply the smell of her arousal, cloying and honey sweet. Jared's gaze was so hot that Ananda did not even have time to be self-conscious of her half naked state. She sat up slightly, crossing both arms at her chest in order to pull her shirt and bra off enjoying the hitch in Jared's breathing as he stared at her newly uncovered body.

Enjoying the gaze on her and yet wanting more, Ananda pawed weakly at Jared's clothes before demanding, "Clothes off." She managed to unbutton his jeans before his brain rebooted and he helped her rid him of the offending jeans and shirt. Ananda got a very brief eyeful of Jared's naked body: his toned flat stomach that lead to thickly muscled thighs and the long hard cock between them that stood almost begging for Ananda's attention. It was as if Ananda was seeing Jared for the first time. True that she had already had him inside of her, but from this angle she truly got an idea of how big the man was and her mouth watered at the sight of him. She pushed the man until he was on his side before sliding down to get a better view of the thickness she longed to have inside of her. Her hand curled around Jared's impressive length and she breathed in deep the scent of citrus and musk that she had come to associate as 'Jared'. She could see that his length was already slick at the tip, his head flushed a dark red color. Without waiting to see what the man would do, Ananda leaned further down to lap at the warm head, humming as his taste burst out across her taste buds.

Jared fought hard not to let his hips thrust with the first feeling of Ananda's tongue against his swollen prick. One of his hands reached down to comb through her hair, not pushing but just holding on and enjoying the woman's explorations. Looking down Jared could see a hint of a smile on Ananda's lips before she dipped down and took him in a bit further, her hands covering what little she couldn't fit into her mouth. Her cheeks hollowed as she expertly provided suction with every withdrawal. It wasn't long before he was close to the edge, cock being expertly worked and stimulated with every thrust of Ananda's sinful mouth and the noises of enjoyment she couldn't seem to contain. Shifting slightly to grip Ananda under the arms, Jared pulled her back up the bed and once again cuddled in close, propping himself up on an elbow. He looked down at the woman who had changed him and leaned in to kiss her again, stroking one large hand along her heated cheeks.

Ananda could still taste the slick from Jared's hard cock and it made her feel warm and alive. She felt no shame in her enjoyment as she sought to give her body what it craved.

"I want you to fuck me, Jared."

The man's hips jerked, clearly liking the idea of once again being buried in her tight sheath. "That's kind of intense baby. Remember you were in a lot of pain afterwards last time." Jared's fingers slid down her side pulling her leg up until it rested across his hips. This gave him access to the source of her biggest pleasure and Jared wanted to make sure he gave Ananda everything before taking his own enjoyment. Reaching back down, Jared enjoyed hearing a hitch in the woman's breathing as one finger slid along her slick folds.

"I wasn't in pain Jared, I was just a bit sore," Ananda answered breathily as her hips began to shift in time with the man's finger. "You are the biggest I've ever had…so far anyway." The last part of her sentence was accompanied by a smirk that made the man want to growl. Instead he slid two fingers inside of Ananda's heated core with no warning, causing the woman to arch back with a pleasured yell.

"The biggest you've had so far, eh? You planning on finding someone else to fill you up like I do baby?"

Jared curled his fingers slightly knowing exactly where to press to see Ananda shiver with spiking arousal.

"Well, first you should definitely put your dick in me," Ananda chimed breathlessly trying to shift in order to get the man's fingers to press deeper into her. To her chagrin, Jared sat up splaying one arm effortlessly over the woman's hips in order to keep her from moving. Ananda never thought her fantasies included being pinned down and ravished to within an inch of her life, but obviously she was wrong.

"Fuck, please fuck me Jared!" Ananda was just trying to rile Jared up with her teasing. There would never be anyone else who could fill her up and make her want like Jared. Just the thought of the man driving his hardened cock into her was enough to make Ananda drip steadily with arousal. Jared swallowed deeply and Ananda was so distracted that she almost missed Jared's next words.

"I know, God I want you too baby. I just don't want to rush this. I want us to take our time and really explore…" Ananda's hand came up and harshly slapped itself across the man's mouth effectively cutting him off.

"I know you want to make every moment we have together special Jar, and I promise next time we can go as fast or as slow as you want. You can tie me up and play with me for hours or use my mouth to get off. Whatever you want okay baby? But next time. Right now I need you to get inside me as quickly as possible until I can't even remember my own name—,"

"A gag would be pretty useful for you as well," Jared interrupted, his thumb moving to circle around Ananda's sensitive clitoris. The feeling has her shuddering deep and Jared groaned at feeling her silky channel contract around his finger.

"That's fine, whatever you want Jared just—," Ananda started to babble until Jared abruptly slid his fingers from her quivering sheath. The feeling of being so fucking empty made Ananda keen with want and she swore she could feel her aching hole pulsing with the need to be stretched and filled by Jared once again.

The man pushed Ananda slightly until she was on her back, legs spread as far as they could go before he settled in between, cock just resting outside her pulsating channel. Jared's dick nudged at the inside of her thigh and what was left of Ananda's brain went completely offline. She whined as her fingertips dug into the skin of Jared's upper arms, begging him without words to end her torture. The man leaned down until his mouth was right next to her ear. "Like this?" He murmured using one hand to prop him up and the other the guide the head of his cock until it rested just at Ananda's greedy, wanting entrance.

"Yeah," she said, mind gone elsewhere as her body did nothing but respond to its own needs.

"Lift up. No, lift your hips. Yeah there you go baby."

Ananda obligingly lifted her hips and Jared shoved a pillow under her lower back before turning all of his attention back to her. "Stop me if it hurts okay? I know you want it, but I'm big and I don't ever want to hurt you."

Ananda opened her eyes and smiled. Her hand slid along Jared's skin until it rested on his stubbly cheeks. "Your dick is big yeah, but it isn't like a monster or any—" She forgot to finish her sentence when Jared began pressing forward. Her entrance offered up a small token of resistance before surrendering gracefully and soon Ananda realized that Jared's cock was firmly nestled within her. For just a second the feeling was almost too much, too alien and then when Ananda thought the feeling would consume her alive, she opened her eyes and looked up. When her and Jared's eyes met, it was as if the room they were in fell away and all that was left was the pleasure between them. Her limbs almost felt as if they were getting looser and Ananda marveled at how new and wondrous sex felt with Jared.

The man shifted and a slow spark slithered up Ananda's spine. Jared leaned down for another toe-curling kiss and Ananda closed her eyes again to lose herself in the feeling of closeness and safety that was making love to Jared. She ran her fingers through the man's soft thick mane and down his neck, the desire to touch him everywhere making her slightly frantic with its presence. When he started to move, her hands gripped onto his shoulders tightly, causing a groan to flow from his mouth and into her own.

The slow drag of Jared's cock sent sparks along Ananda's spine and she shivered with the feeling. "Jared," she sighed, back arching slightly. The man leaned down to nuzzle the soft skin of her neck, leaving small open-mouthed kisses that made Ananda's breath puff out unsteadily. He kept his rhythm steady and unhurried, basking in the feeling of finally being close to another person without worrying that they would betray him in the morning. The feeling of joy at being buried deeply in Ananda's body threatened to shake tears from Jared's own eyes and his brow furrowed slightly with concentration focusing on keeping his pace steady and not being too much of a sap.

Ananda had no such qualms about her emotions and freely let the tears fall from her eyes and wet the pillow underneath her. Reaching up, she buried her hands in Jared's hair and tugged him up until their mouths met again, wet and uncoordinated. "Jared please…" Ananda arched her hips up with the next thrust making them collide with more force. Somewhere inside of her, a light turned on zapping her nerve endings and pushing her closer and closer to the precipice of her desire. She pushed up against him, trying to make him quicken his pace and moaning loudly between dirty wet kisses.

Despite Ananda's pleas, Jared's pace never quickened and it drove her almost mindless with lust. Soon she was moaning with every thrust and begging loudly for Jared to end his torturous pace. "Just Jared! I need it, need you. Please harder, fuck me harder."

Jared's eyes darkened as his hips sped up, pausing occasionally to push in deep enough that Ananda's gasps turned into whimpers, her fingers going into spasms against the moist skin of Jared's back. Her toes began to curl with each snap of the man's hips and

Ananda scrambled to get a better grip on Jared's sweaty shoulders. A few solid thrusts later and Ananda's back arched one last time as her channel tightened around Jared's now pulsing length. For a moment Ananda could swear she'd gone blind, her mind and her body seemingly disconnected with the force of her climax. When she came back to herself, she could hear Jared moaning her name, his hips thrusting erratically as he chased his own release.

Reaching up to once again tangle her fingers in his hair, Ananda focused on tightening and releasing her still sensitive core as she crooned in his ear. "Fuck me Jared. Come inside me and fill me up. Give me everything," she demanded, nails scraping against the man's scalp and making him shudder. When the man continued, his movements were less fluid with no rhythm. He ground against Ananda until his body tightened and he was flung head first into his climax.

Ananda couldn't help but stare at Jared's face, the face of the man who had come to her when she hadn't even known she needed him and gave her the feeling she had been chasing for so many years. Afterwards, they lay together, legs entwined within tangled sheets and Jared's slowly softening cock still nestled inside of her. The feeling of Jared's warm come sliding out of her is one that Ananda had never thought she would like but knew she would never be able to live without. She knew without a doubt that one day, when they were safe from the people who were hunting them, they would try undeterred by birth control until they made a child: with sharp cheekbones, amber eyes and thick dark hair.

When Jared finally slipped from her body, Ananda stood and entered the bathroom to get some warm towels to clean themselves off. The feeling of now cooling come sliding down her thighs was not one that she was even remotely comfortable with and so she set about changing that. Ananda could hear shuffling in the room and paused suddenly with the feeling that they weren't alone. Suddenly she heard a quiet knock at the door followed by a voice she never thought she'd hear again.

"I know Ananda is here. We all need to talk."

Wrapping a towel hastily around herself, Ananda rushed from the bathroom and came face to face with her brother and…

"Kerri?"

To be continued in Book 5

If you enjoyed this title, I would appreciate your leaving a review of the book. Good reviews encourage an author to write as well as help books to sell. Good reviews can be just a few short sentences describing what you liked about the book without having a spoiler. If you could spend 30 seconds writing a review, I would appreciate it: you can review this title right now at your favorite retailer.

Here is a preview of the **next story** you may enjoy:

Evasion - The Mind Talker Paranormal Romance Series, Book 5

JARED FELT anything but relaxed as he sat across from the man who just introduced himself as Ananda's older brother. Typically, he would assume a first meeting with the family of a significant other would include a semi-awkward dinner with the father asking all sorts of probing questions followed by pseudo threats of death by shotgun if a hair on his darling daughter's head was out of place. Instead Jared sat gingerly on the edge of a raggedy bed, clothes having been hastily pulled on in the wake of their new company, with Ananda sobbing in her big brother's arms. A big brother who somehow managed to be comforting to his sister while his eyes promised swift and sudden death to Jared if he found she had come to any harm.

Ananda missed the exchange between her brother and Jared as she pulled back, tears in her eyes and a sob stuck in her throat. Truthfully she had thought she would never see Ryan again and was a bit perplexed by his abrupt re-entry into her life. Her gaze was drawn to how close Ryan and Kerrie were as well as the feeling of raw magnetism that almost radiated between them. Slowly, she backed away until Jared guided her down until she was almost perched across his lap, his arm never leaving the place where it was draped across her waist in a possessive and comforting hold.

"I'm…" Ananda, swallowed hard pushing down the lump in her throat. "It's been months, Ryan. Months! One minute you're telling me about your exploits in the real world; job, house, car, everything. The next you just up and disappear with no phone calls, no emails, nothing!"

"I know Ana and I'm sorry, I really am but," Ryan paused, his gaze sliding over to Kerri as if needing her permission to speak the truth. Ananda could feel her fury rising over her brother and best friend's seemingly unspoken exchange. "We wanted to keep you safe –"

"Keep me safe?!" Ananda exclaimed incredulously. "Were you keeping me safe when you let mom and dad send me to all those shrinks and specialists who made me feel as if I were crazy for hearing voices? Were you keeping me safe when you abandoned me and moved halfway across the country the first chance you got?!" Ananda's voice rang out shrilly as she stood abruptly, fists balled and barely hanging onto what little sanity she had left after the past few days.

"Ananda I know," Ryan started only to be cut off again by his sister's angry voice.

Fighting against Jared's tightening hold around her waist, Ananda could feel fresh hot tears spilling from her eyes and racing down her flushed cheeks. "No you don't Ryan. You don't know shit about anything, especially not how I feel. And you," Ananda turned to the woman she had loved as a sister sitting stock still and unsurprised by Ananda's ire. Her unusual calm almost made Ananda want to rage even harder. "I thought you were my friend and now it seems you'd been lying to me too. How long have you two been plotting and spying on me, huh? Did you have a good laugh at my bumbling efforts to figure out who I was? I should have known something wasn't right when you never invited me to meet your family!"

At the mention of her family, Kerri's countenance changed and her words rang out with a fury greater than Ananda had ever witnessed from the redhead.

"My family is the reason why our lives are so fucked right now!" Kerri used her hands to say the word family in quotations as if the very idea of family was somehow ridiculous. "The reason I've never invited you to meet them is because I washed my hands of them years ago." The slight woman stood abruptly and began pacing as if unable to speak the words while staying still.

"When I was fifteen, my mother, younger sister and I moved to New York. I thought it was strange that my father and brothers didn't come with us, but I figured he had a good reason and didn't dwell on it, instead focusing on school and making friends and trying to be popular." Kerri stopped, turning slowly to look at Ryan, emotion clear in her eyes. "And then I fell in love."

Blinking, Jared looked between the two guests. Without even trying, he could feel the love and affection that practically pulsed off of the two in waves and wondered if he and Ananda were exuding similar feelings.

"I'm so confused right now," Ananda whispered plopping down beside Jared once again. She leaned against him heavily and gladly soaked up the feelings of calm the man was radiating out. She would have had to be a fool to not see the depth of feeling between her brother and Kerri, but it still didn't explain how they knew each other or why they were here now. And how did they even find them?

"I called Bill, whose real name is apparently Ryan and he is also, apparently, your brother," Jared answered.

"Wait," Ananda spoke up. "Didn't you say your friend Bill was in Canada? Wasn't he the guy with safe houses?"

If you enjoyed this sample then look for **Evasion - The Mind Talker Paranormal Romance Series, Book 5**.

Here is a preview of **another story** you may enjoy:

The Siren's Trap - The Daemon Paranormal Romance Chronicles, Book 4

PHOEBE STARED out at the ocean. In La Coruna, or A Coruna as the locals called it, the ocean was everything. Next to her was the world's oldest lighthouse. It was said to have been built by Hercules himself in ancient times. After several weeks of being in Spain and an excellent grammar book, she was finally starting to pick up on the language. Right now was not the time for studying. This moment was hers alone to stare into the great expanse of ocean before her. Across those waters, she had helped to search for a new leader, find the Qilin, and fell in love.

Already, memories were starting to float back into her mind. The spiteful witch, Juno, had taken her memories temporarily. As memories of Supay started to flow back, Phoebe realized why. Juno was not intent on leading daemons to take over the world or even gain power. They had overestimated her goals. From everything that Phoebe could figure out, Juno just wanted to cause trouble. She thrived on causing hurt to people. Although Juno had agreed to stay out of the infighting, she had managed to split Supay and Phoebe apart. Now, Phoebe was across the world with Apollo. He had rented a condo near the beach and spent each day trying to prove his love. At first, his attempts had been endearing. Now, it felt like he was smothering her. In reality, nothing may have been different. She had just started to change as her memories came back. Phoebe remembered Supay's cute quirks and his dedication to always doing what was right. She also remembered her own disapproval of Apollo and his intention to kill the Qilin. Alone at the edge of the world, there was no escape from her memories.

Picking her way down the rocks, Phoebe got as close to the ocean as possible. The few tourists that were there spoke Spanish, since La Coruna was a Spanish-tourist destination. On occasion, she ran into the random English family who had decided to take holiday there. The number of English speakers that she had met could be counted on one hand. It made for a lonely existence, but she felt less alone as her Spanish improved. The warmth of Spain and the salty sea air were a welcome change from the thin air at Cuzco.

Sitting down on a rock, Phoebe started to cry. Since finding out she was pregnant, her hormones had gone haywire. It did not help that she truly was in a bad situation. She was stuck in Spain with Apollo and could not bring herself to tell him that she was pregnant. Since she was only a few months along, it still was not noticeable. Even worse, she could not bring herself to call Supay and tell him that she was going to have their child. Unless Supay stopped by the cabin, he may not even know that she was gone. Even worse, he may have already realized she was gone. If so, he would be frantic with worry.

If you enjoyed this sample then look for **The Siren's Trap - The Daemon Paranormal Romance Chronicles, Book 4**.

Here is a preview of **another story** you may enjoy:

Alpha Packed: A BBW Paranormal Shifter Romance - Book 4

DARLENE DREAMT of immense power. She controlled any spirit that passed by her. They would bend to her will and do whatever she requested. The thrill of it made her feel more alive than she ever had before, even if she was in the world of the dead.

Then someone tugged on her skirt. Darlene looked down to see a young boy. She had seen him before, in a dream over a month ago, calling out to her. He looked normal enough, with blond hair cut close to his head and big blue eyes. He wore a torn, muddy soccer uniform.

"He's coming," the boy warned.

Darlene frowned and reached out for him, but he slid through her fingertips like water. He faded away, leaving her alone.

Darlene's eyes opened slowly. A loud noise can be heard from outside her apartment. She could hear people talking. Groggily, she looked over at her alarm clock, which showed it was a little past eight in the morning. She had hoped to get another couple hours of sleep in before the start of her shift at the bookshop.

She rubbed her eyes, thinking back to the dream she had. The dreams were growing more vivid lately. Darlene was starting to think they weren't even dreams but something more. Maybe she truly was in the other world while she slept. She decided she'd have to see Rosamund and ask if that was even possible.

Darlene sat up and was surprised to see the drowned woman peeking into her room. She only left the bathroom in times of emergency. Her milky white eyes made Darlene wish she could go back to bed.

Instead, she asked, "What is it?"

Darlene knew almost nothing about the drowned woman. She was hesitant to speak and was loyal to Darlene because she could see her and interact with her – apparently saving her from a terrible life of no one ever seeing her roaming spirit again. Her clothes were too ruined for Darlene to think of any time period that they could belong to. She had decided not to pry into the drowned woman's old life and merely accept the fact she had a roommate who lived in her bathroom.

"Your neighbor was killed," the drowned woman told her.

Darlene frowned. The apartment next to her on the right was empty, which meant… Her eyebrows shot up. The other apartment was home to the old lady who was constantly and consistently a pain in Darlene's ass. She would gripe about any and all noises Darlene made and threatened to call the police on a daily basis. However, lately, she had been bragging about having a boyfriend, which seemed to thrill her.

Darlene began to get out of bed. "Are you serious? Do you know anything else?"

"The body is unsightly."

Darlene didn't want to know what that meant. She put her hair up hastily and tugged a sweater on. It was winter now and even though the sun was out, it was sure to be chilly. Darlene opened the door to the hallway and found a swarm of police officers as well as paramedics.

One of the cops saw her and tried to block her from going into the old woman's apartment. "Ma'am, please step back inside your home."

"What happened?" Darlene asked, playing dumb as best as she could.

"Ma'am, please, go back inside."

Darlene tore her gaze away from the front of the old woman's apartment and looked at the young officer. "Is she okay?"

"Ma'am, an officer will be by to question you later. Please go back inside until this area is all clear."

The paramedics left the woman's apartment, carrying out the stretcher, which had a white sheet over it. Darlene's heart pounded. She was transfixed. The police officer was irritated, trying to get her back into her apartment. As Darlene took a step back, the old lady's hand slid out from under the sheet, and Darlene's breath caught in her throat. Along her wrist were bite marks – clearly a vampire's.

"Fine, I'm going," she snapped suddenly, stepping back into her apartment and shutting the door, catching her breath.

The drowned woman floated over to her, concern on her features. "Did you see the corpse?"

"I saw her wrist. Vampire bite marks. What did you see?"

The woman looked sad. "Wounds that matched those of one given by a werewolf."

Darlene felt as if her heart was going to pop.

"When I said get a normal job, I didn't mean here with me." Maria looked at Idris, her thick glasses making her eyes look like an insect's.

Idris shifted his weight uncomfortably. He hadn't thought this all the way through. That seemed to be his biggest problem regarding everything. His wrist began to itch, which it did whenever he was stressed and was being reminded of his own Exsul status. Maria never seemed to be bothered by her own Exsul tattoo, but she had been Exsul a lot longer.

That was the entire reason why Idris started visiting Maria. It had been two months since the debacle with Atticus, Liara and Darlene. In one fell swoop, he had blown up everything in his life.

His relationship with Darlene had crumbled and burned in front of his eyes, by his own hand. He had pushed her away and then lashed out in such a disgusting manner that she was now dating Mark, the leader of Roman's old pack.

Atticus, the man who had Changed him, a maggot on the planet, had somehow infested his way back into Idris's life. Idris had let him and the fault was with him. Atticus promised him a pack, which was the only thing Idris wanted back. Instead, he lost all sense of himself and who he was. He had ended Atticus's life, but at that point, the damage had been done.

Liara still treated him with respect, which Idris felt he didn't deserve. Yes, he had stopped Atticus from killing her, but he still had gotten upset when she refused to support their Exsul pack idea. As Idris recovered in the hospital, Liara had come to see him and said that she forgave him. She was forever a better person than he was. Before Liara left, she told Idris to forgive himself and work to be a better person.

Idris had taken her words seriously. The first thing he had done once he got out of the hospital was get out of that disgusting motel room he had been holed up in since Lucian went missing. He rented a small bachelor's pad on the opposite side of town, away from Darlene, in case he suddenly felt like seeing her. The next thing he did was take Darlene's advice and went to see Maria.

Maria had been an Exsul for a long time and used magic to hide herself from other werewolves, although it hadn't been strong enough for Liara. Idris had treated her like trash when he had found out about her Exsul status, something he had been too embarrassed to admit. But Maria was able to make a life for herself outside of the pack, now owning a book store that specialized in books no one wanted. If she could be content as an Exsul, why couldn't he?

"Speak up, boy." Maria crossed her arms – she was always tough on him, but in a motherly way that Idris never had as a kid.

"I don't have enough experience to get hired anywhere else," he mumbled, abashed.

"What did you do for work before this?"

Idris shrugged. "I fixed cars whenever I was able to find the work. Sometimes I protected people, like a body guard. Before all of this happened and I was second-in-command to Lucian, I helped him run his hardware store."

"So go work at a hardware store."

Idris cringed. "I…tried. The interview didn't go so well."

Understatement of the year. When the guy interviewing him role played as a difficult customer, Idris found himself irritated until he finally told the guy to Google what he wanted if he didn't want to listen to him.

Maria sighed, her bangles on her wrists clattering together. "Idris, you know why I don't want you working here."

He did. Darlene still worked here and having an ex-couple working together was something that made Maria nervous. It made Idris nervous, too, but there was no way anyone else would hire him with a blank resume where all his references were dead or paranormal.

"Can't I work in the back?"

"The back? You mean the closet where we put extra books?" Her face softened. "I'll ask around for you, okay?"

"Thanks, Maria."

"What are your plans for today?" It was the daily question she asked him, either by text or in person, to try to get Idris's head on straight.

"I planned on going to go to the library. Read there. Try to relax. I used to like to read. As a kid, I mean. Before everything happened."

Maria nodded in approval and opened her mouth to speak when the door to the bookshop opened. Idris turned around and saw Darlene fly in. Idris tried to control the way his heart beat quickly when he saw her. *You messed up and you don't deserve her*. He prepared himself for Darlene's glare when she saw him, but she barely glanced at him as she ran up to Maria.

"Jacob," she breathed. "He's back."

Maria stiffened. Idris's breath caught in his throat. Jacob – Lucian's vampire/werewolf hybrid who had escaped the night Lucian was killed. There had been no sign of him. Idris assumed Lucian's plan had failed and Jacob was dead somewhere. Darlene recounted the story quickly, ending with what her ghost had told her. Maria paced the floor.

Idris spoke first, although he loathed to do so. "Didn't she…" He realized he still didn't know her name.

"Gertrude, apparently," Darlene answered for him.

"Didn't Gertrude have a boyfriend recently?"

He hadn't wanted to bring that up, for the mere fact that Gertrude was the reason Idris had found out about Darlene running to Mark. But if that stirred up any memories for Darlene, it didn't show on her face.

"That's right. You don't think it could be Jacob, do you? I never saw him around but…Who else would be close enough to get to her?"

"Were there any clues in the apartment that could have been left for you?" Maria asked.

Darlene shrugged. "If so, there was nothing overt. Otherwise the cops would have been all over me again, like with Rebecca."

Idris chewed on his lip, thinking. "The only other person who was in on Lucian's plan was Vivica. And has anyone seen her lately?"

Darlene and Maria shook their heads. Idris hadn't seen her either, not since the night that Darlene had to stake Rebecca and Vivica had been so consumed with getting Idris back she had orchestrated his battle with Roman. There hadn't been any peep from her since.

While that was a blessing, it was also worrisome. Vivica was not one to stay idle for long. Idris hadn't thought of her much since Atticus and the aftermath, but now that Jacob was back, a sick feeling formed in his stomach.

"I'm going to look for her in the catacombs," he said. "Maybe your ghost can help you get into Gertrude's apartment?"

Darlene nodded. "Good idea. I should wear gloves though, shouldn't I? I don't want anything of mine left at the crime scene."

Idris looked at Maria, who nodded gently at him to go and find Vivica. He zipped up his jacket, getting ready to go out in the cold. As he walked toward the door, Darlene called to him. He stopped.

"Be careful."

"You, too."

He headed out toward his truck.

If you enjoyed this sample then look for **Alpha Packed: A BBW Paranormal Shifter Romance - Book 4.**

Other Books by Darla Dunbar

- The Romeo Alpha BBW Paranormal Shifter Romance Series

- Romeo Alpha Blood Lines Romance Series

- The Alpha Feud BBW Paranormal Shifter Romance Series

- The Alpha Packed BBW Paranormal Shifter Romance Series

- The Daemon Paranormal Romance Chronicles

- The Leather Satchel Paranormal Romance Series

Get the latest update on new releases from the author at:

https://darladunbar.com/newsletter/

About the Author - Darla Dunbar

Darla has been interested in paranormal romance since she was a teenager in high school. It was then that she discovered she could fulfill her fantasies through her writing.

Observing people and human behavior in the area of romance has always been one of her favorite pastimes. Combining that with an overactive imagination is a sure fire way of coming up with interesting themes.

Connect with Darla Dunbar

I really appreciate you reading my book! Here are my social media coordinates:

Friend me on Facebook:
https://www.facebook.com/darladunbar/

Follow me on Twitter: https://twitter.com/DarlDunbar

Check me out on Goodreads:
https://www.goodreads.com/author/show/8425857.Darl a_Dunbar

Subscribe to my newsletter:
https://darladunbar.com/newsletter/

Visit my website: https://darladunbar.com/